For Phil
~*JW*

For Pamela & Robin
~*GR*

First American edition published 2000 by
Crocodile Books, USA
An imprint of Interlink Publishing Group, Inc.
99 Seventh Avenue • Brooklyn, New York 11215 and
46 Crosby Street • Northampton, Massachusetts 01060
Published simultaneously in Great Britain by Little Tiger Press,
an imprint of Magi Publications, London
Text © 2000 Judy Waite • Illustrations © 2000 Gavin Rowe
Library of Congress Cataloging-in-Publication Data
Waite, Judy.
The Stray Kitten / by Judy Waite ; illustrated by Gavin Rowe.
– 1st American ed.   p. cm.
Summary: A stray kitten learns how to survive on the streets until he is
rescued by a little boy.
ISBN 1-56656-356-9 [1. Cats–fiction.] I. Rowe, Gavin, ill. II. Title.
PZ10.3.W134 St 2000 [E]–dc21 99-048499
For a complete range of Crocodile illustrated children's books,
please write to us at the above address, call us toll-free at
1-800-238-LINK, or visit our website at **www.interlinkbooks.com**

THE *Stray Kitten*

BY JUDY WAITE
ILLUSTRATED BY GAVIN ROWE

Crocodile Books, USA

An imprint of Interlink Publishing Group, Inc.
NEW YORK

He was just a scrap of a kitten,
living among a heap of old pipes
and thorn bushes at the edge of the road.
It was a rough, hard life, and he was always
hungry.

    Sometimes he hunted insects or small
creatures. Sometimes he found bits of food
tossed lazily away by the people that wandered
past. But he didn't pounce on the food.
He circled it slowly.

He had learned to be watchful.

One day some children came by. They were fun to play with at first, but after a while the kitten grew tired and crept inside the pipes.

The children shouted and wiggled sticks at him, but he didn't come out again. At last they got bored and went away—all except the smallest boy. He sat by the pipes, calling softly. But the kitten didn't move or make a sound.

He had learned to be quiet.

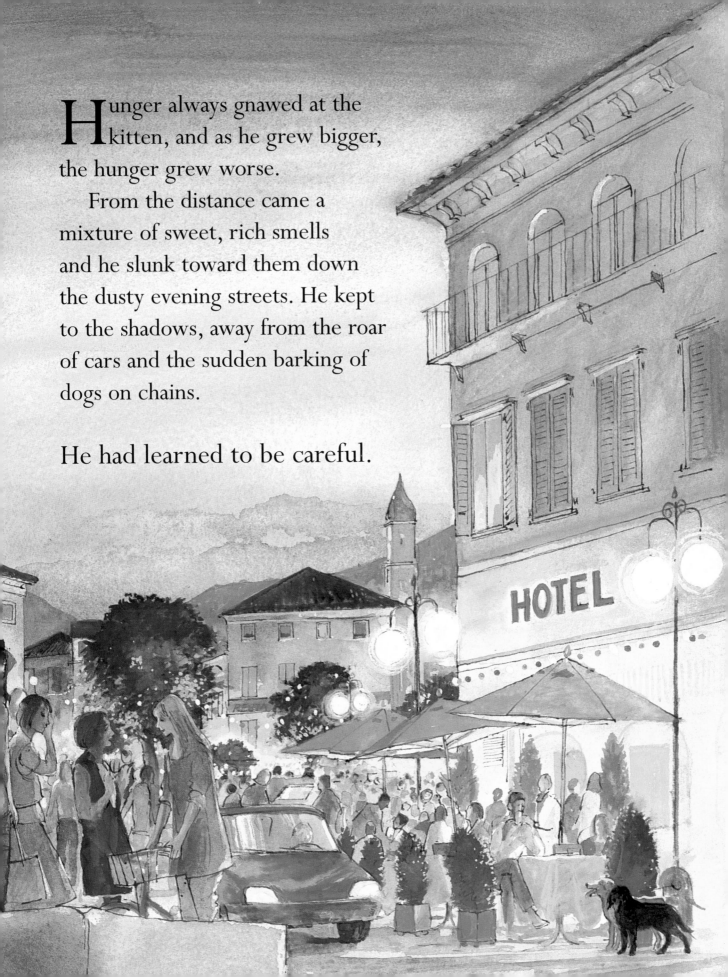

Hunger always gnawed at the kitten, and as he grew bigger, the hunger grew worse.

From the distance came a mixture of sweet, rich smells and he slunk toward them down the dusty evening streets. He kept to the shadows, away from the roar of cars and the sudden barking of dogs on chains.

He had learned to be careful.

The place of rich, sweet smells was lit with a hundred tiny lights. The kitten crept softly among the forest of chairs and tables.

The smells drove him crazy, but he slid into the shadowed space between tubs of summer flowers and waited. His sharp green eyes watched carefully. His tail twitched, and his whiskers quivered, but he stayed hidden.

He had learned to be patient.

When food was thrown out at the end of the evening, other cats rushed out of the shadows. The kitten rushed with them, and a small boy tossed him scraps of fish. The sweet taste sang in his mouth.

The other cats were jealous. They arched and hissed, they spat and clawed. But the kitten arched and clawed back.

He had learned how to fight.

After that, the kitten followed the smells every night, growing bigger and stronger on the scraps of people's meals. He was not a kitten any more.

But there came a night when no more people sat eating outside. Instead, the wind whipped the cloths from the tables, and the sea flung itself angrily against the shore. The young cat sat for a long time, watching the door where the food had come from.

He had learned to be hopeful.

The young cat's stomach twisted from thoughts of food. In desperation, he leaped onto the window ledge, calling loudly to the people inside.

Suddenly the door was flung open and a shouting woman hurled a bowl of cold water at him. The cat fled in panic. He would not cry by windows again.

He had learned to be wise.

As the days passed, hunger tore at the cat. At night he
roamed through wind-torn gardens, clawing at the
bags of rubbish. He would eat anything, however bad it
smelled, however rotten it tasted.

But even as he scratched and scraped in his desperate search, he was always ready to run from danger.

He had learned to be quick.

The weather grew worse. Most of the houses were empty and shuttered. No rich, sweet smells ever filled the air. No bags of rubbish appeared in the gardens. And among the rain-lashed grass and scraggly bushes no small creatures or insects stirred.

The cat lay, thin and cold, inside the damp, rusting pipes and hardly moved. He was weak and tired.

He had learned not to care.

One morning, very early, the cat was woken by an angry rumble. He heard voices and shouting. The ground heaved and shook. Everywhere the air roared, and in terror he flattened himself against the rattling pipes. Something enormous was crashing down upon him. His fur rose and his eyes were wild.

He had learned about fear.

uddenly, someone was reaching for him. The cat was
lifted and carried gently into a garden, past a window,
and through a door. He was too weak to struggle. At first
he crept to a dark, low place and wouldn't come out.

But sweet, rich smells were drifting toward him.
He sniffed the air, remembering. Then slowly, nervously,
he moved toward the smells and began to eat.

He had learned to be brave.

As the warm air slipped back into the days, the cat grew strong and healthy. Sometimes he lay in the garden, lazily watching the insects. Sometimes he caught the muddled smells of people and scraps and places with a hundred lights. But he never slunk through the shadows to find them. He was quiet enough to be petted, patient enough to be cuddled, brave enough to be stroked.

He had learned to be loved.